THIS BOOK BELONGS TO

"Tonya M. Huffman's *Spreading the Gossip* is a must read for any child, teenager, or adult. Her writing style is very much geared toward her target audience—young people—but her message reaches out to all ages. 'Doing what's popular isn't always what's right, and doing what's right isn't always what's popular' is a lesson that we all need to be reminded of. I wish that some of our politicians would read this story. Perhaps they will! I hope Ms. Huffman will write more short stories for young people, because children today can use all the help they can get."

- Dug Ward, *Manager, Faculty UCLA Animation Workshop*

"*Spreading the Gossip* is a unique book that presents the dangers of gossiping. This book will help all children learn the valuable lesson of not to gossip."

- Melissa Neal, *M.D.*

"*Spreading the Gossip* convicts the heart of anyone who has participated in gossiping. It opens the eyes of everyone who has tried to 'fit in.' I recommend this book for all ages and for studying in school and in the church."

- Felisa Eafford, *Upward Bound Director, Cuyahoga Community College*

"In a day and age when America's youth are gaining popularity by becoming pop stars and committing immature acts, the message that *Spreading the Gossip* presents is a perfect example for our children to follow. All children and their parents should read this. It's a simple read, but it teaches a powerful message."

- David Patterson, *Owner PRstore Honolulu, & Broadcast Producer*

"In the engaging book *Spreading the Gossip*, Tonya M. Huffman crafts a simple story to which children and adults can easily relate, and it exposes the real harm that gossiping can cause."

- Dave Cockley, *Children's Author, Playwright, and College Professor*

To my father, mother, and brother, respectively Larry, Terries, and Brian for always believing in me and supporting me in all of my positive endeavors, even when I doubted that storms would clear the sky so that I would have an opportunity to fly. Also to those relatives, educators, and acquaintances who always knew that I would soar. Thank you all.

Published by Tate Publishing & Enterprises, LLC
127 E. Trade Center Terrace | Mustang, Oklahoma 73064 USA
1.888.361.9473 | www.tatepublishing.com

Tate Publishing is committed to excellence in the publishing industry. The company reflects the philosophy established by the founders, based on Psalm 68:11,
"The Lord gave the word and great was the company of those who published it."

Book design copyright © 2008 by Tate Publishing, LLC. All rights reserved.
Cover design & interior design by Elizabeth A. Mason
Illustration by Jason Hutton

Published in the United States of America

ISBN: 978-1-60462-851-7
1. Juvenile Fiction   2. Social Situations: Values
3. Ages 7-12   4. Christian
08.02.13

SPREADING THE

GOSSIP

TONYA M. HUFFMAN

Tate Publishing & Enterprises

FOREWORD

I always remember being taught the Golden Rule, which says, "Treat others as you want to be treated." I also remember being taught that "Silence is golden." And still I remember learning, "If you don't have something nice to say about a person, don't say anything at all." These adages have stuck with me from the time I learned them, and they are still very much a part of my life today. I also learned, in both religious settings and in school, the value of monitoring what one says. In religious settings, I learned that humans are blessed with two ears and one mouth, so we should listen more than we talk. In school, teachers often brought up that the words *silent* and *listen* have the exact same letters rearranged, so we should be silent when we listen.

As an educator who is also a loyal Christian, Tonya teaches, tutors, and instructs students not only by imparting essential subject matter, but also with how to be civilized humans in society. In this book she shows readers how gossiping can bring even a well-respected person to disgrace. This book suitably teaches children and adults alike that gossiping is inappropriate, and it is a must read for anyone who can and has ever communicated with anyone. Enjoy this teachable, entertaining, and engaging book.

Robert T. Noll
John Carroll University
Communications Professor

C larice, a student at Christian Academy Elementary School, had a lot going for her. She was friendly, talented, and extremely intelligent. But Clarice was not satisfied.

larice wanted to be popular like the "in crowd" girls. These girls were stylish, cliquish, and, pitifully, they gossiped about people. Desperate to gain their approval and be popular, Clarice began gossiping with them. In the morning, she gossiped in academic classes. This was the beginning of worse to come.

In the afternoon, Clarice had Bible class. In Bible class, she had several friends. On days when wearing uniforms was optional, her friend Allan dressed eccentric and often told Clarice about his dream to become a fashion designer. Nadia, with long hair always rolled up in a bun, played dolls with Clarice and fixed the dolls' hair stylishly. And it was shy Ryan who loyally listened whenever Clarice talked to him about anything.

For no other reason but to fit with the "in crowd," Clarice began to gossip about her friends with others in Bible class. Clarice joked, "Allan dresses so weird that he could blend in well with clowns at a circus." She continued to spread the wisecracks. "Nadia styles dolls' hair better than her own. She always wears that bun on her head. That's so played out," Clarice joked.

Clarice even wrote a note dishonestly pretending that it was from Ryan, where a complaint was made to the Bible schoolteacher Miss Shepherd about how bored he was in class. Clarice really got out of hand with gossiping.

Miss Shepherd made an announcement to the class. "Tomorrow someone will receive an award for being the most knowledgeable student in Bible class. This person was chosen based on having the highest quiz scores and participating in meaningful class discussions," she said.

During break, Clarice snuck the note that she'd written from Ryan into Miss Shepherd's desk drawer. Then she gossiped to her friends and others in class about the unknown student who would be honored.

"This student is probably not that smart. Miss Shepherd shouldn't give awards like this," said Clarice. She kept gossiping. While most made no response to her comments, many defensively encouraged her to cease the idle talk.

After break, Miss Shepherd put students in groups to complete an assignment. Clarice was placed with Nadia and Allan. She needed to share a book with Nadia and borrow a pencil from Allan. They told Clarice how ridiculous rumors had gotten and how bad her gossiping made them feel. They didn't give her much conversation. Clarice felt guilty, for the same people she gossiped about were the same ones who shared with her.

When Clarice headed home, she realized that being popular at the expense of losing friends and suppressing guilt wasn't worth anything. To have gained approval from the popular girls, something she wanted for so long, Clarice was not satisfied.

The next day during Bible class, Miss Shepherd made an announcement. "Due to a conflict, Ryan will no longer be in our Bible class; he has been transferred to another teacher," she said. Many wondered what the situation was between Ryan and Miss Shepherd. Then Miss Shepherd said, "It is now time to honor the student who will receive the Most Knowledgeable Award. The recipient is Clarice!"

Just then, half the class clapped for Clarice while the other half silently observed. With a regretful look, Clarice reluctantly walked to the front of the class. After a long pause, she said, "Miss Shepherd, I cannot accept this award." Miss Shepherd and half the class looked at each other puzzled. Clarice continued, "I want to apologize for sowing discord. In efforts to be accepted by a popular crowd here at school, I began gossiping about my friends, and it was I who falsely wrote the note claiming that Ryan was unhappy in this class. Furthermore, I even downed you, Miss Shepherd, for wanting to reward a student as Most Knowledgeable, and I downed the student who would receive this award, who, coincidentally, was me."

Miss Shepherd went to her desk, took out a container of bubbles, and handed them to Clarice. She told Clarice to open the bubbles and blow them. Clarice was puzzled, but did as asked. When Miss Shepherd stopped Clarice, she said, "Blowing bubbles represents gossip that flows from ear to ear. The popped bubbles represent the damage gossip creates. Once the bubbles pop, you can't recreate them. Thus, it is seldom easy to repair damage caused by words."

Then Miss Shepherd had all students get in a circle. She told Clarice to whisper a message to the person beside her, and eventually it would be whispered from person to person, around the circle. "I see tulips on a lawn," Clarice whispered to her neighbor. After the last person whispered the message back to Clarice, Clarice said out loud, "I see two lips on a fawn." Clarice realized that this was not her original message. Miss Shepherd said, "This game called Telephone illustrates that gossip can get distorted when passed along, often resulting in wrong messages being sent and received. The class and I accept your apology, Clarice, but hopefully you learned your lesson. And remember, doing what's popular isn't always what's right, and doing what's right isn't always what's popular."

Clarice said, "I truly learned my lesson. I learned that gossip harms and, more importantly, it makes me feel guilty, especially when I depend on these same people for favors. Again, I sincerely apologize to everyone."

Miss Shepherd still gave Clarice the award. Then she said, "Clarice, I am going to appoint you as my Bible school assistant where you'll use your gift of gab to help me teach lessons and perform other classroom duties. Helping to spread what's in the Good Book is always in order."

From that day forward, Clarice used her gift to help teach and promote good. While assisting Miss Shepherd, she looked around and saw all of her friends, including Ryan. She was glad to have made amends with them; Clarice was finally satisfied.

e|LIVE

listen|imagine|view|experience

AUDIO BOOK DOWNLOAD INCLUDED WITH THIS BOOK!

In your hands you hold a complete digital entertainment package. Besides purchasing the paper version of this book, this book includes a free download of the audio version of this book. Simply use the code listed below when visiting our website. Once downloaded to your computer, you can listen to the book through your computer's speakers, burn it to an audio CD or save the file to your portable music device (such as Apple's popular iPod) and listen on the go!

How to get your free audio book digital download:

1. Visit www.tatepublishing.com and click on the e|LIVE logo on the home page.
2. Enter the following coupon code:
   f9f1-0fa4-8af6-cfb5-564b-a274-bdea-1935
3. Download the audio book from your e|LIVE digital locker and begin enjoying your new digital entertainment package today!